key to reading™

At Key Porter Kids, we understand how important reading is to a young child's development. That's why we created the Key to Reading program, a structured approach to reading for the beginner. While the books in this series are educational, they are also engaging and fun – key elements in gaining and retaining a child's interest. Plus, with each level in the program designed for different reading abilities, children can advance at their own pace and become successful, confident readers in the process.

Level 1: The Beginner
For children familiar with the alphabet and ready to begin reading.
- Very large type
- Simple words
- Short sentences
- Repetition of key words
- Picture cues
- Colour associations
- Directional reading
- Picture match-up cards

Level 2: The Emerging Reader
For children able to recognize familiar words on sight and sound out new words with help.
- Large type
- Easy words
- Longer sentences
- Repetition of key words and phrases
- Picture cues
- Context cues
- Directional reading
- Picture and word match-up cards

Level 3: The Independent Reader
For increasingly confident readers who can sound out new words on their own.
- Large type
- Expanded vocabulary
- Longer sentences and paragraphs
- Repetition of longer words and phrases
- Picture cues
- Context cues
- More complex storylines
- Flash cards

Max and Morris were
playing superheroes.

Max was Super Bunny.
Morris was Zoom Zoom.

Ruby and Louise were blowing up balloons.
There was a small yellow one, a big blue one
and an even bigger red one.

Ruby hit the red balloon.
It floated away!
"Uh-oh," said Ruby.

Max zoomed into the kitchen.
He caught the red balloon.
"Super Bunny!" said Max.

Morris zoomed into the kitchen.
"Zoom Zoom!" said Morris.

Ruby took the red balloon back.
"We need these balloons," she said.
"We're making a solar system."

"The smallest balloon is going
to be the moon," said Louise.
Ruby pointed to a picture of the moon.

"The bigger balloon is going
to be the earth," said Louise.
Ruby pointed to a picture of the earth.

"The biggest balloon is going
to be the sun," said Louise.
Ruby pointed to a picture of the sun.

"Now please zoom away," said Ruby.
"We don't want you to break the balloons."

"Super Bunny!" said Max.
"Zoom Zoom!" said Morris.
Together they zoomed away.

Ruby and Louise glued paper to the balloons.
Some paper got glued to their faces!

Ruby and Louise painted the moon grey.
They painted the sun yellow.
They painted the earth blue and green.

Ruby tried to put the earth on a hanger.
But she tripped over Max's red lobster.
The earth went flying in the air!

Max and Morris zoomed into the kitchen.
Max caught the earth!
"Super Bunny!" said Max.

"Thank you, Super Bunny," said Ruby.
"Thank you, Zoom Zoom," said Louise.

"You saved…"

"The world!" said Max.